SUKI
The Very LOUD Bunny

Carmela & Steven D'Amico

DUTTON CHILDREN'S BOOKS
An imprint of Penguin Group (USA) Inc.

For Burgin and Jena Utaski

And with "infi-infi" thanks to Olivia, who thought of Suki first

DUTTON CHILDREN'S BOOKS
A division of Penguin Young Readers Group

Published by the Penguin Group • Penguin Group (USA) Inc., 375 Hudson Street,
New York, New York 10014, U.S.A. • Penguin Group (Canada), 90 Eglinton Avenue East,
Suite 700, Toronto, Ontario M4P 2Y3, Canada (a division of Pearson Penguin Canada Inc.)
• Penguin Books Ltd, 80 Strand, London WC2R 0RL, England • Penguin Ireland, 25
St Stephen's Green, Dublin 2, Ireland (a division of Penguin Books Ltd) • Penguin Group
(Australia), 250 Camberwell Road, Camberwell, Victoria 3124, Australia (a division of Pearson
Australia Group Pty Ltd) • Penguin Books India Pvt Ltd, 11 Community Centre, Panchsheel Park,
New Delhi - 110 017, India • Penguin Group (NZ), 67 Apollo Drive, Rosedale, North Shore 0632,
New Zealand (a division of Pearson New Zealand Ltd.) • Penguin Books (South Africa) (Pty) Ltd,
24 Sturdee Avenue, Rosebank, Johannesburg 2196, South Africa • Penguin Books Ltd,
Registered Offices: 80 Strand, London WC2R 0RL, England

Library of Congress Cataloging-in-Publication Data

D'Amico, Carmela.
Suki, the very loud bunny / Carmela and Steven D'Amico. — 1st ed.
p. cm.
Summary : Unlike most bunnies, Suki loves shouting and playing
in the mud, but when she disobeys her mother and leaves the burrow
one day, her loud voice is what saves her.
ISBN 978-0-525-42230-3 (hardcover)
[1. Rabbits—Fiction. 2. Behavior—Fiction.] I. D'Amico, Steven. II. Title.
PZ7.D1837Su 2011
[E]—dc22   2010013470

Published in the United States by Dutton Children's Books,
a division of Penguin Young Readers Group
345 Hudson Street, New York, New York 10014
www.penguin.com/youngreaders

Designed by Sara Reynolds
Manufactured in China • First Edition
10 9 8 7 6 5 4 3 2 1

Everyone knows that bunnies are soft, fuzzy, shy little creatures who spend their lives hopping through fields, nuzzling veggies, and barely making a sound.

Of course, there are always exceptions.

"Suki, we mustn't call attention to ourselves,"
Momma said, hushing her. "We're bunnies.
And bunnies never shout."

"Sorry, Momma," she said.

Suki was just excited. It had rained the night before, and the whole world was covered with gigantic sparkling puddles.

"Suki!" Momma gasped. "Bunnies do *not* splash in the mud. Our coats stay shiny and clean. Run along now and eat your breakfast."

Happily wet and muddy, Suki hopped to her breakfast of dandelion greens.

"I LOVE dandelion greens!" she announced.

Her brother Mickey teased her. "Well, you don't have to shout about it, Suki."

"I WASN'T"—she started to shout—"shouting," she finished softly.

While she ate, a butterfly fluttered by and circled around her head.

Suki hopped as high as she could and spun and twisted and hopped again, pretending her feet were wings.

"Look at me!" she shouted. "I'm a butterfly. I'm flying!"

"Suki," Momma said, sternly this time.
"I've had just about enough. We're bunnies and
bunnies don't fly. We hop. So hop along, both of
you, now. We're gathering carrots for lunch."

Suki and Mickey hopped through the field that
ran alongside the burrows, looking for carrots.

"Come on," Suki said, when they reached the edge
of the field. "Don't you want to see what's out there?"

"It's the great big world," Mickey said. "And
Momma says bunnies should stay in the burrows."

Suki was tired of hearing about what bunnies should and shouldn't do.

"We better . . . you better not," Mickey called as she hopped away.

Mickey didn't know what he was missing.
The great big world was amazing! There
were dozens of butterflies to fly with, more
dandelion greens than she could *ever* eat, and
the most gigantic and sparkling puddle that
Suki had ever seen.

She rushed toward the puddle . . .

. . . and jumped right in.

But this was no ordinary puddle. The fast-moving water pushed her farther and farther away from home.

Finally, Suki grabbed the side of a rock and clung with her all strength.

She climbed on top and drew a deep breath. Springing high into the air, she flew like a butterfly to safety.

"That was kinda scary," she said, flicking her wet coat dry. Was that why Momma had told her *no jumping in puddles?*

She decided she'd better get back to the burrows, before Momma got worried or Mickey told on her—or both.

Which way were the burrows again?

Twitching her nose, Suki smelled carrots—
the burrows must be near! She hoppity-hop-
hop-hopped and sniffed and followed the
wonderful scent until she came upon the biggest
carrot she had ever seen.

YUM! Suki thought.

Her tail twitched in excitement.

Then everything went dark.

Oh no! Suki was trapped!
She hopped to the left and the right—trapped!

TRAPPED!

Suki bounded forward, but she couldn't see what was in front of her.

Suddenly there was a crash,

and she tumbled into the light.

Even though she was still very hungry, she ran away from that dangerous carrot as fast as she possibly could.

She *had* to get home, before Mickey told on her, or Momma got worried, or both.

Suki searched all afternoon, until the sun sank
into the grasses. Surely Momma would look for her
soon if she wasn't looking already. But the great big
world was so very big, how would she ever find her?

Suki was so tired her eyes began to close. She was almost asleep when she heard a rustling sound in the nearby bushes.

"*Momma?*" Suki whispered. "Is that . . . is that you?"

The something sounded big. And the something was getting closer.

"Momma?" she said, a little more loudly.

Suki was suddenly frightened and wished more than anything that she was at home in her cozy bed with her momma kissing her good night.

Suki shouted as loudly as she could. She shouted so loudly her whiskers shook, so loudly the leaves of the maple tree swooshed, so loudly a beetle had to cover his ears, and SO loudly that very soon . . .

. . . Momma's voice was whispering behind her.
"There, there, Suki, darling," she said.
"I'm here."

"Suki," Momma said, "for once I'm glad you didn't stay quiet. How else would I have found you?"

Suki's eyes brightened. "Does this mean I get to shout from now on and splash in puddles and fly?"

Momma laughed. "We'll see about that."

Suki told her brothers and
sisters everything that had happened.
Huddling in their beds, they hung
on her every word.

Soon, her brothers and sisters were quiet.
The night was quiet. The burrows were quiet.
Sometimes, quiet is nice, Suki thought.
"Good night, everybody," she whispered.

"GOOD NIGHT, SUKI!"
everybody shouted.